My Pet Died

Written and Illustrated by

Rachel Biale and _____
(your name)

TRICYCLE PRESS
Berkeley, California

Remembering our dog, Papageno

Acknowledgements

Many thanks to Nicole Geiger for her sensitive, thoughtful editing,
and to Brenda Leach for her keen eye and charming design.

TRICYCLE PRESS
P.O. Box 7123
Berkeley, California 94707

Illustrations by Rachel Biale
Book design by Brenda Leach/Once Upon a Design

First Tricycle Press printing, 1997
Manufactured in the United States of America

1 2 3 4 5 6 — 01 00 99 98 97

Why Make a Book About It?

The *Let's Make a Book About It* series offers you a unique and powerful tool for helping your child cope with difficult and challenging experiences. Making a book together helps your child master the powerful, often sad or scary emotions the experience evokes. It also enables you to elicit, validate, and support your child's feelings.

All you need to make a book with your child is a pair of child-safe scissors, paste or tape, assorted crayons, felt tip pens or colored pencils, a camera (optional), old magazines, this book, and *time*. It can be a lot of fun and a wonderful keepsake, as well as an invaluable coping aid. For a young child, the process of making a concrete object by cutting and pasting, drawing, dictating, and writing is much more helpful than reading a ready-made book. A ready-made book, as helpful as it may be, can leave your child with a sense of how one "ought to feel," while a book made by your child truly validates whatever your child feels. In addition, the open-ended nature of a *Let's Make a Book About It* book allows your child to express genuine, uncensored feelings in a creative way and at her own level. Often, the book you make together will become a cherished possession—like a security blanket or beloved teddy bear—that magically contains feelings of attachment, caring, and support. You'll probably find that your child wants to read the book over and over and will return to it for nurturing and support at other difficult or challenging times. However, some children may use the book as a way of finishing and putting away the distressing feelings brought about by a difficult event, and that is fine as well.

Why It Is Important to Deal with the Death of a Pet

For many children, this will be their first encounter with death. For such a child, the pet's death may carry the trauma of the first realization of the meaning of death and grief. For children who have already experienced the death of a family member or a friend of the family, the death of a pet will often reawaken feelings of loss and pain. Parents or guardians may be surprised, even upset, to see their child more shaken by the death of a pet—even "just a goldfish"—than they were about the death

Cut out these pages if you wish.

of a member of the family, but this is very common for young children. It is important for you to realize that the death of the pet becomes a way for children to re-experience and deal with feelings about other losses, such as other deaths, injuries, illnesses, difficult separations, or moving to a new home.

It may be very hard to see your child in emotional pain. The first and natural reaction of parents is to say "Don't cry," or try to rush in to "kiss it and make it better." Inadvertently, we may try to minimize the child's pain by offering to get a new pet, distracting the child with presents or fun activities, or making statements such as "It's only a goldfish!" It is important for you as a parent to let your child have feelings of sadness and anger and let him know that you understand and are with him in his grief. If you rush to "make it all better," you give your child the impression that having and expressing grief and anger is not okay.

When a pet dies, a child usually feels sad, angry, and confused. She needs clear and concrete information about death, emotional support, and her parent's or guardian's understanding of the depth of her feelings. As sad and scary as the death of a pet may be for your child, it creates a very important opportunity for learning for the first time or reworking how to deal with loss, and for explaining the nature of death. Unlike the death of a person in the family, the death of a pet, in most cases, is an experience of manageable emotional proportions for a young child. While the child may love the pet dearly, the attachment is not the same as to a person and the death of the pet will most likely not be as devastating to the adults around her as the death of a person would be. In addition, while for some children the loss of a pet is a terrible one—the pet may have been their best friend—a child is not dependent on the pet for her fundamental physical and emotional needs, as she is on a parent, grandparent, guardian, or other close family member. The clear distinction between an animal and a person helps lessen a child's fear about her own or her parents' deaths. Finally, after an appropriate period of grieving, a pet can be replaced by a new one and most children will soon form a new, healing attachment.

You can be most helpful to your child by recognizing and validating how powerful his feelings are. A funeral for the pet, even if it was a gecko or a beetle, is very important. The size, cost, or personality of the pet should not be an important consideration; your child's attachment to the pet and his emotional reaction to the recognition of the reality of death is what matters. Talking about the feelings and letting your child know it is all right to be sad and not feel better right away is what the child will find most helpful.

Finding ways to talk to your child about death may be hard for you. Use the guidance offered at the end of this book for suggestions on how to explain it. Give your child, and yourself, plenty of time to deal with the death—do not expect your child to be over it in a day. However, if your child seems sad, angry, or otherwise upset for a long time, the pet's death may be triggering other unresolved fears or grief and should not be ignored. Generally, the younger the child, the shorter the grief period. If a toddler or preschool child is visibly upset or depressed for more than two or three weeks, or an elementary school-age child for more than a month, you should seek professional guidance. See the sections "Recognizing Signs of Stress in Children" and "What to Do About Children's Stress" at the back of this book.

Making a Book About the Death of a Pet

Making a book together after the death of a pet will provide an important tool for your child in coping with painful and confusing emotions. Putting feelings and thoughts into a concrete object with you will allow your child to feel mastery over her emotions, while being comforted by your support. This book will become something that "carries" feelings of grief and eventually allows your child to feel a sense of closure and to move on. Importantly, this book will also provide you with guidance in addressing your child's feelings and explaining death.

As you make the book together, be attentive to the words you use to encourage your child to describe his feelings and draw in the book. Stay away from words that suggest judgment of these feelings, such as "good" and "bad." Instead, try using statements such as "I can see that you really are sad" or "I know it's hard to feel sad and angry." Always assure your child of your love as you talk about these feelings. Let him know that feelings of sadness, fear, and anger are as acceptable as the more upbeat feelings. Remember, when you talk to very young children about their artwork, it is important to use open-ended comments such as "Tell me about this" rather than "What is this a picture of?" You'll be surprised how much your child, in his imaginative way, can see in what, to you, is a scribble. Ask your child if he would like you to write down what he tells you.

When you talk with your child about what has happened to her pet remember that more than anything else, a child needs reassurance that you understand her feelings and that you'll be there to take care of her. Any experience of death will raise some worries for your child about your death and her safety. Try to be reassuring without saying that you will never die. For example, you may say something like "I expect to live for a very, very long time—until you are a mommy, maybe even a grandma, and I'll take care of you as long as you need me."

As you make this book together with your child, remember to be open to and accepting of your child's feelings and worries. Gently correct misunderstandings and try to calm his fears but do not do so by minimizing his feelings. The most help you can offer your child is "being there" to hear his feelings and thoughts. You do not need to "fix" and make everything better. You can also share some of your feelings or childhood memories of death and loss as long as you do so in moderation. Be careful not to unload your feelings onto your child in a way that makes him feel he has to take care of you.

This book is very open-ended. Take the instructions on each page as suggestions and starting points. You can adjust the book to your child's age and needs; skip the pages that do not seem to interest your child. However, this book has been designed with the psychological process of dealing with death in mind, so try to at least mention all the issues raised by it.

If you have more than one child who would benefit from making a book, it is best if each child has her own book (this is especially true for twins). If this is not possible, ask your children how they would like to work on the book together. For example, you could draw a line splitting the page into two equal halves, or combine ideas, drawings and pictures on a page.

As you make the book together, do not rush! The book is meant to be worked on for several weeks. Allow your child to do as much as he can in the book by himself, from the cutting and pasting to coloring and writing. Do not worry about the pictures looking nice. A child's jagged cutting of a picture or messy scribble all over the page is much more meaningful to him than your neat work. Finally and most importantly, be sure that "making a book about it" is first and foremost a time for warmth and closeness for you and your child.

Further Help

In addition to making a book together about the death of your pet, encourage your child to talk to family members, friends, and trusted adults as well as to express herself through play. Play is children's primary way of expressing and working out their feelings. Do not be alarmed if your child plays "dying and funerals" for a while—it is a helpful process. You can facilitate it by providing an empty shoe box and some paper or cardboard for a coffin and grave stone. A small "memorial corner" for the pet set up in the house may be helpful, too. There are further suggestions for helpful activities at the back of the book.

You may wish to cut out these introductory pages before you start making this book with your child. It will make the book more your child's and less yours.

My Pet Died

by _____

This is me: _____.

Have your child paste his or her picture and write his or her name on the page (with your help, as needed).

This is my family, the _____ family.

(family name)

Paste in a picture of the family. In separated, divorced, and blended families, be sure to include both sides of the family, and any pets still living. Encourage your child to draw the family and write or dictate everyone's names.

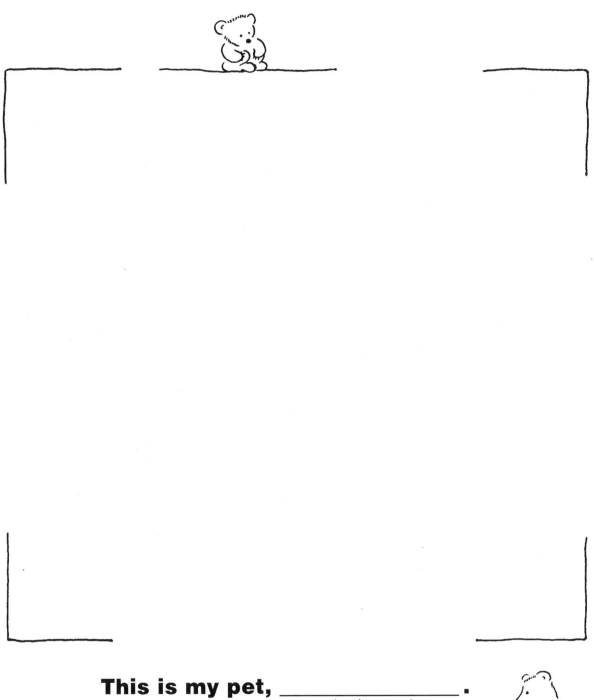

This is my pet, _____ .
(pet's name)

Paste in a picture or have your child draw the pet, and write the pet's name on the line.

But _____ died. This is what happened:
(pet's name)

_____

_____

_____

_____

Have your child write or dictate the story of how and where the pet died (at home, at the vet, etc.) If the pet has disappeared or you don't know where it died, have your child still give the place some name such as "somewhere out in the world" or just your town's name. Gently provide your child with explanations and information needed to understand the cause of death, and encourage your child to draw a picture about it. The drawing does not need to be realistic; you can suggest drawing how it *feels,* rather than exactly how it happened.

This is what happened to _____'s body:

(pet's name)

_____

_____

_____

_____

Have your child write or dictate what happened, such as a burial in a pet cemetery or cremation or burial by the vet. If you have a choice, it is preferable from a young child's point of view to bury the pet (even in an unidentified grave) than to cremate it.

Thinking about _____ dying

(pet's name)

makes me feel _____

_____

_____

_____

_____

_____

_____

_____

Have your child write or dictate the feelings on this page and then illustrate them on the facing page with a drawing or pictures. (Illustrations could include magazine clippings or self-portraits.)

Continue on this page with your child's feelings.

Other people in my family feel _____

_____

_____

_____

_____

_____

_____

_____

_____

_____

 Tell your child how you feel and write it down. Interview everyone in the family and have them either write in the book themselves or dictate their feelings to your child or to you.

Continue with feelings and statements from everyone in the family. Call grandparents (or other extended family members to whom your child feels close) and have them dictate their thoughts over the phone.

I think dying means _____

_____

_____

_____

Have your child write or dictate what he or she thinks death means. (Hold your input until the next page.) Then have him or her use drawing and magazine pictures to illustrate these concepts, even if indirectly. For example, if your child focuses on the body stopping its functions, a picture of an animal lying down can do. If the focus is on some concept of "going to heaven" let your child choose how to illustrate it (for instance, a picture of a beautiful sky, a rainbow, or an abstract design).

My parents told me dying means _____

_____

_____

_____

_____

_____

In simple, clear concepts tell your child how you see death. This is a good time to talk about your religious or spiritual beliefs, or a naturalist-biological view of death. Write it down and illustrate with a drawing or picture. You may want to use an abstract drawing or picture rather than a literal one. Consult the section at the back of this book, "How to Talk to Children About Death," for guidance.

Other people told me about dying that _____

_____

_____

_____

_____

_____

Ask your child whom he or she might want to talk to outside the family to get more information about death. This could include a teacher, a clergy member, the vet, or a trusted friend or neighbor. When you go to talk with these people, take the book along so you or your child can write or draw in it. This is an important part of the process for your child—it involves sharing the news about the pet's death and learning that it is okay to talk about death and ask questions. It also shows your child whom to turn to outside the family.

From books I learned that dying means _____

_____

_____

_____

_____

Have your child write or dictate what he or she may have learned from books about death. (For suggested titles see the reading list at the back of this book.) Illustrate with your child's drawing.

These are other things that I know have died:

_____

_____

_____

Have your child write or dictate a list and illustrate with drawings and pictures. The list can include animals and plants, characters in stories or movies, etc.

These are people I have known
(or know about) who have died:

_____

_____

_____

Have your child write or dictate names of family members or other significant people in your child's life who have died. If your child is fortunate and has not experienced death in the family you can either skip the page or mention names of grandparents or great grandparents that the child did not know. Have your child paste their photos or draw a picture below the names.

This is the story of _____'s life.
(pet's name)

Have your child write or dictate the story of the pet's life from the time you first got the pet. Illustrate with drawings or photos of your pet at different stages. If you do not have photos of the pet use pictures from magazines. Continue on the next page as necessary.

Continue the pet's life story on this page.

This is what I liked most about _____:

(pet's name)

_____

_____

_____

Have your child write or dictate his or her favorite things about the pet. Illustrate with drawings, photos of the pet (if possible), or pictures from magazines of animals doing similar things.

This is what I used to do with _____:
(pet's name)

_____

_____

_____

Have your child describe and draw himself or herself with the pet doing things such as feeding, going on walks, and playing.

I know I will be sad for a long time, maybe as long as _____.

Have your child draw and write or dictate about the length of the grieving process. Your child can illustrate this with an abstract drawing or collage, by making a calendar, or by referring to other experiences of time passing.

I think I'll start feeling better when

_____

_____

_____

_____

_____

Have your child speculate about and then write or dictate what events or passage of time will occur before he or she starts to feel better. A lot of children will say "When I get a new pet." It would be wise to acknowledge the feeling but not rush to do it. Your child needs the time to feel sad and grieve. Ask your child if he or she would like to draw or paste a picture of him or herself looking happy, but do not push it—some children will not be ready yet.

Here are some things I can do to help myself when I am sad and I miss _____:

(pet's name)

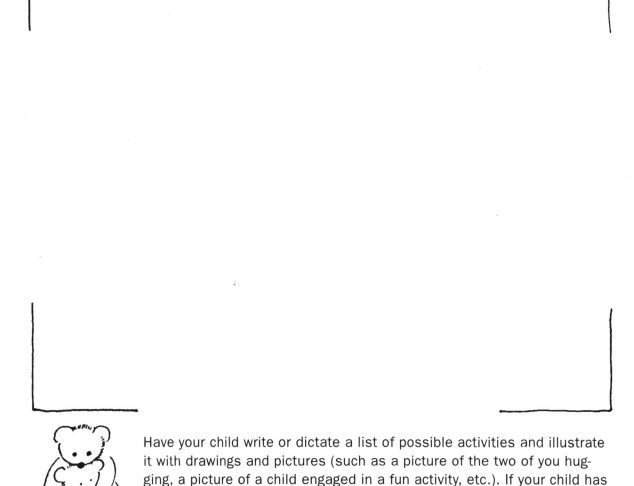

Have your child write or dictate a list of possible activities and illustrate it with drawings and pictures (such as a picture of the two of you hugging, a picture of a child engaged in a fun activity, etc.). If your child has few or no ideas, you can offer suggestions. (See "Suggested Activities After a Pet Dies for Kids and Parents" at the back of this book.)

Here are the people I can talk to
when I am sad and I miss _____:

(pet's name)

_____

_____

_____

Have your child write or dictate names of people to talk to, and draw or paste in their pictures.

If I could talk to _____ I would say
(pet's name)

_____

_____

_____

_____

Have your child write, dictate, and/or illustrate what he or she would say to the pet. Encourage the inclusion of words of farewell.

Continue the farewell activity from the previous page.

Maybe some day I'll get another pet.

It may be a _____

_____

After some time has passed and you have had a chance to work on all or most of the pages up to this point, have your child write or dictate a list of possible pets and paste in their pictures from magazines. If you are certain that you do not plan to get another pet, skip this and the next page.

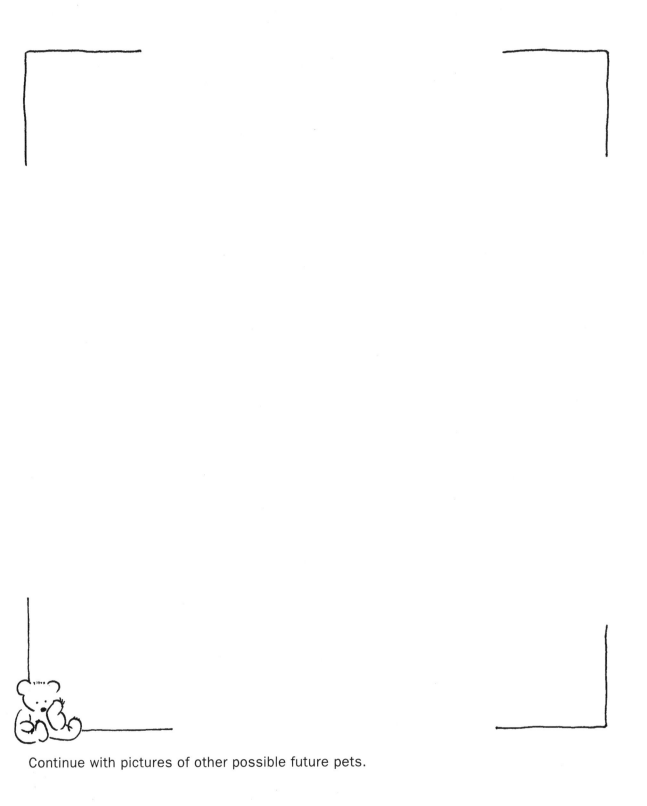

Continue with pictures of other possible future pets.

A long time has passed. Now I feel

_____

_____

_____

About two to four weeks after you've begun work on this book (the older the child, the longer you should wait), have your child write or dictate these feelings and draw a picture to illustrate them.

This is what I would tell
other children whose pets die:

_____

_____

_____

_____

Have your child write or dictate words of advice to other children.
Illustrate with your child's self-portrait (a drawing or photo) or even
a picture of someone teaching children.

How to Talk to Children About Death

Before you talk to your child about death, you might want to consider what, if anything, makes you upset or uncomfortable about death or about talking to your child about it. You may find that your own experiences of death—or perhaps the secrecy with which it was treated when you were a child—get in the way of a comfortable, clear discussion. You may also need to clarify to yourself what it is that you believe about death and what you want your child to know. Give yourself some time to come to terms with your own feelings and ideas about death before you talk to your child. Talking to family members, friends, your child's teachers, or a rabbi or minister may be helpful first steps.

Begin by listening to your child's feelings and to your child's questions. Try to stay focused on what it is that your child wants to know rather than on giving your child a comprehensive picture. Your child will ask you about the things she needs to understand for coping with her immediate experience. Too much information can be confusing and overwhelming.

Try to provide concrete explanations and use clear language. Stay away from vague expressions like "passed away," "gone," or "departed." Words that refer to ordinary activities like "going" or "leaving" may be scary to a young child who takes them literally, not euphemistically. He may begin to associate any ordinary departure with death! Be especially careful not to equate or associate death with sleeping or going to the hospital because your child could draw the conclusion that if he goes to sleep or to the hospital, he might die.

Begin your explanation of death by describing what happens to the body in terms such as: "When a pet dies its body does not work anymore. It does not move, does not breathe, does not eat. . . ." If your child knows about internal organs, you can explain that the heart no longer pumps blood. Adjust the level of sophistication to your child's knowledge and questions.

If you want your child to believe in an afterlife, begin by giving an explanation of your concept of a soul or an "inner part." For example: "We have feelings and thoughts that are not exactly like our inside body parts but are inside us. These continue after the body parts don't work anymore." Then you can add whatever your vision is of where that "inner part" goes after death. To some, it may be to Heaven; to others, it is into the memories of the living.

Give your child a simple, concrete explanation about why we bury people and pets. Incorporate the idea that a grave lets us put the body in a special place that we will always remember. If your pet is very small, you may want to ask your local Health Department about burying it in your backyard or in a nearby nature area. Mark the grave with stones or a plant. This will  be helpful for your child and she'll probably feel comforted that the pet has a "resting place." If your pet died at the veterinarian's office, find out about what was done with the body. If you have the chance to make a choice, burial is preferable to cremation and a known grave is preferable to an unidentified site. If it's not possible to visit the grave, describe it in a concrete way such as "on a special hillside by some big trees." You can embellish the information you get from the vet a bit, but don't overdo it.

Encourage your child to express a wide range of feelings about the death including sadness, anger at the pet or at other people in the family, loneliness, wishing the pet could come back "at least one last time," guilt (usually expressed by thoughts like "if only I had/had not . . . the pet would not have died"), as well as feelings of resentment and a desire to not talk about it. Some children generalize from the experience of a pet's death and become worried about themselves or their parents. Be reassuring about your child's safety and your health and expectations of a long life, but do not promise that you will never die.

Some children become more angry than worried, and they need understanding and acceptance. However, do not let anger "spill over" into violent behavior or the breaking of household rules. An angry child needs the reassurance of familiar rules and of you staying clear, firm, and in charge.

Encourage your child to talk about the pet's special qualities, including what he liked about the pet, what he used to do with it, what he'll miss the most, and how he'll remember it. A child who seems especially bereft by the death of a pet may need some guidance and reassurance about where he will get the love and friendship he felt for and from the pet. Suggest his family, friends, and other caring adults. If your child seems really resistant to talking about the pet's death, give him more time. While you wait for him to be ready, give him extra hugging, holding, and quiet times of closeness with you. Reassure him that when he is ready to talk, you'll be ready to listen. Put this book on a shelf where he can see it, and let him know that he can get to it when he is ready.

Suggested Activities After a Pet Dies for Kids and Parents

• It is very helpful, when possible, to have a funeral for the pet, or some kind of memorial or farewell ceremony if a funeral is not possible. Let your child create the ceremony on her own and do not be offended if she uses religious language or rituals she has experienced elsewhere that may seem sacrilegious to you.

• Make a poster about the pet's life as a kind of "goodbye card" for the pet. The poster can be taken to school or friends' houses for sharing, and displayed at home. Your child can also ask other people who knew the pet (neighbors, family, and friends) to write something on the poster.

• Create a little "memorial corner" for the pet either where it lived in the house or near its favorite spot. The pet's picture, a flower, its toy or favorite food are all appropriate mementos for such a special spot.

• Your child may want to write a letter to other children whose pets have died. Give the letter to the vet for display, or to copy and hand out in the vet's office.

• Create a written or oral series of stories about the pet (such as "The Legend of Rex") featuring adventures the pet would have in a fantasy land. Take your cue from your child as to whether or not he wants to be in the story as well.

• Ask your child if she wants to visit friends' or neighbors' pets, and perhaps, if appropriate, give them any food left over from your pet. Some children will find this very helpful while others will not be ready to part with the pet's things.

• If your child wishes to go see animals at a pet store or zoo, it can be helpful—but do not rush to do so.

• Read books together about the death of a pet or death in general. Choose those books that do not dictate to your child how he ought to feel. Some suggested titles are:

Lifetimes, Bryan Mellonie (Bantam, 1983)

About Dying, Sarah Bonnett Stein (Walker & Co., 1984)

The Tenth Good Thing About Barney, Judith Viorst (Aladdin, 1987)

Recognizing Signs of Stress in Children

Confronting death can be a very upsetting experience for both children and their parents. The following is intended to help you recognize signs of stress in young children and in your family as a whole. The common symptoms of stress listed below can make you feel frustrated, angry, and worried about your child. Try to remain aware of your child's increased needs and the knowledge that the symptoms are usually temporary.

The symptoms of stress can often be seen through regression, physical complaints, and emotional disequilibrium. Parents should watch for the following signs:

• Regressing to earlier behaviors such as toileting accidents, thumb sucking, needing a bottle, baby talk, and wanting to be carried.

• Clinging to parents and "love objects" (such as a special blanket, stuffed animal, or pacifier) and difficulties with separations. Also, resisting going to school or friends' houses, and expressing increased fears and anxieties.

• Sleep disruptions: waking up in the middle of the night, resisting bedtime, needing more parental companionship at bedtime, wanting to sleep in the parents' bed, nightmares and night terrors.

• Physical complaints: stomachaches and headaches are the most common. Other symptoms are loss of appetite and vague complaints about feeling sick along with unusual tiredness and excessive reactions to minor injuries.

• An increase in temper tantrums, aggression, and wildness appears in some children, while others become withdrawn and lethargic or show little or no feeling. Children may express their loss by complaining of boredom and by finding it hard to initiate play. Some show difficulty in concentrating and sustaining their play activities, or seem fidgety and unfocused.

• Increased conflicts with parents and siblings, angry outbursts, and provocative oppositional behavior are very common.

What to Do About Children's Stress

Offer your support by making this book, trying the other suggested activities, keeping your daily life simple and your routines consistent, and expressing your certainty that your child will soon feel more at peace with the loss and more upbeat. Especially with regressive behaviors such as toileting accidents, maintain a balance between assuring your child that the behavior is a common reaction to change and difficult times, and expressing your certainty that your child will soon regain control and feel as much a "big boy" or "big girl" as before. If signs of stress persist beyond 2–3 weeks in young children (under 5) or up to a month in older children, or if your child has so many difficulties that your family life is severely disrupted, it is recommended that you get additional help. Consult a professional (such as a child or family therapist, a pediatrician, or a teacher) for more support and guidance.

More books for families that can help...

We Are Moving
Rachel Biale
This first book in the interactive *Let's Make a Book About It* series is designed to help families with young children adjust to moving to a new home. Ages 4 to 8, 48 pages, paperback

Who's in a Family?
Robert Skutch • Illustrations by Laura Nienhaus
An open-minded picture book featuring single parent-, grandparent-, and same-sex partner-led families, plus some of young children's favorite animal families. Ages 3 to 7, 32 pages, hardcover

Feelings
Inside You and Outloud Too
Barbara Kay Polland, Ph.D. • Photographs by Craig DeRoy
"Makes a useful starting point for adult/child discussions." —*Washington Post*
Includes photos and easy-to-read text. Ages 4 to 8, 64 pages, paperback

The Parenting Challenge
Practical Answers to Childrearing Questions
Barbara Kay Polland, Ph.D.
A reassuring, common-sense guide for families with infants to 12-year-olds which provides creative suggestions for real-life problems. 232 pages, paperback

Nightmare Help
Anne Sayre Wiseman
This book shows how to help children end the cycle of problem dreams. 128 pages, paperback

We Shake in a Quake

Hannah Gelman Givon • Illustrations by David Uttall

At last, a book for young children that not only explains what an earthquake is, but also tells how to prepare for one and deal with the feelings that arise afterward. Ages 4 to 8, 32 pages, hardcover

Hooray for Me!

Remy Charlip and Lillian Moore • Illustrations by Vera B. Williams

All children wonder about their relationships to themselves and to others. This book answers the question: "What kind of me are you?" Ages 3 and up, 36 pages, hardcover

For more information, or to order, call the publisher at the number below. We accept VISA, MasterCard, or American Express. You may also wish to write for our free catalog of books and posters for kids and their grown-ups.

Tricycle Press
P.O. Box 7123
Berkeley, CA 94707
1-800-841-BOOK